# The Trader's Wife

Louis Becke

THE TRADER'S WIFE

By Louis Becke


Unwin Brothers 1901

## CHAPTER I

Brabant's wife was sitting on the shady verandah of her house on the hills overlooking Levuka harbour, and watching a large fore and aft schooner being towed in by two boats, for the wind had died away early in the morning and left the smooth sea to swelter and steam under a sky of brass.

The schooner was named the *Maritana*, and was owned and commanded by Mrs. Brabant's husband, John Brabant, who at that moment was standing on the after-deck looking through his glasses at the house on the hill, and at the white-robed figure of his wife.

"Can you see Mrs. Brabant, sir?" asked the chief mate, a short, dark-faced man of about thirty years of age, as he came aft and stood beside his captain.

"Yes, I can see her quite plainly, Lester," he replied, as he handed the glasses to his officer; "she is sitting on the verandah watching us."

The mate took the glasses and directed them upon the house for a few moments. "Perhaps she will come off to us, sir?"

Brabant shook his head. "It is a terribly hot day, you see, Lester, and she can't stand the sun at all. And then we shall be at anchor in another hour or so."

"Just so, sir," replied the mate politely. He did not like Mrs. Brabant, had never liked her from the very first day he saw her a year before, when Brabant had brought her down on board the *Maritana* in Auckland, and introduced her as his future wife. Why he did not like her he could not tell, and did not waste time in trying to analyse his feelings. He knew that his old friend and shipmate was passionately fond of his fair young wife, and was intensely proud of her beauty, and now, at the conclusion of a wearisome five months' voyage among the sun-baked islands of the Equatorial Pacific, was returning home more in love with her than ever. Not that he ever talked of her effusively, even to Lester, tried and true comrade as he was, for was naturally a self-contained and somewhat reserved man, as one could tell by his deep-set, stern grey eyes, and square jaw and chin.

"Damn her!" muttered Lester to himself, as he stood on the topgallant foc'scle watching the two boats with their toiling crews of brown-skinned natives; "nearly five months since she last saw him, and there she sits calmly watching us as if we had only sailed yesterday. Afraid of the sun! She's too selfish and too frightened of spoiling her pretty pink-and-white skin—that's what it is."

An hour later the boats came alongside, and then, as the chain rattled through the hawse-pipes, Brabant came on deck dressed in a suit of spotless white.

"Shall we see you this evening, Jim?" he asked, as he stood waiting to receive the Customs officer and doctor, whose boats were approaching.

"Thank you very much, sir, but I would rather stay on board this evening, as Dr. Bruce is sure to come into town some time to-day, as soon as he hears the *Maritana* is here, and I should not like to miss him."

"Just as you please, Jim. But why not take a run on shore with him, and both of you come up for an hour or two after dinner?"

The mate nodded. "Yes, we could do that, I think; but at the same time, Mrs. Brabant won't much care about visitors this evening, I'm afraid."

"My wife will be only too delighted, Jim," replied the captain in his grave manner; "you and Bruce are my oldest friends—that is quite enough for her."

The port doctor and Customs officer came on board and warmly greeted the captain of the *Maritana* for, apart from his being one of the wealthiest traders in the South Seas, John Brabant was essentially a man who made friends—made them insensibly, and then his beautiful young wife was the acknowledged belle of the small European community in Fiji, and his house, when he returned from one of his trading voyages, was literally an open house, for every one—traders, storekeepers, cotton planters, naval men or merchant skippers—knew there was a welcome awaiting them in the big bungalow on the hillside at whatever time they called, day or night. Such hospitality was customary in those old Fijian days, when every cotton planter saw before him the shining portals of the City of Fortune inviting him to enter and be rich, and every trader and trading captain made money so easily that it was hard to spend it as quickly as it was made; and Manton's Hotel on Levuka beach was filled night after night with crowds of hilarious and excited people, and the popping of the champagne corks went on from dusk till dawn of the tropic day, and men talked and drank and talked and drank again, and told each other of the lucky strokes they had made; and sun-tanned skippers from the wild and murderous Solomons and the fever-stricken New Hebrides spoke of the cargoes of "blackbirds" they had sold at two hundred and fifty dollars a head, and dashed down a handful of yellow sovereigns on Manton's bar "for a drink all round." And then, sometimes, a long snaky-looking brigantine, with the name *Atlantic* on her stern, and the Stars and Stripes flying from her gaff, would sail into the noisy little port nestling under the verdured hills of Ovalau Island, and a big man, with a black, flowing beard, and a deep but merry voice, would be rowed ashore by a crew of wild-eyed, brown-skinned Polynesians, and "'Bully' Hayes has come! 'Bully' Hayes has come!" would be cried from one end of Levuka to the other, as every one, white, black, and brown, ran to the beach to see the famous and much-maligned "pirate" land, with a smile on his handsome face, his pockets full of gold, and he himself ready for anything or everything—a *liaison* with some other man's wife, a story of his last cruise, a fight "for love" with some recently discovered pugilist of local renown; a sentimental Spanish song to the strumming of his guitar; or the reading of the burial service according to the rites of either the Roman Catholic Church, or that of the Church of England, over the remains of some acquaintance or stranger who had succumbed to fever or a bullet, or Levuka whiskey. Brave, halcyon days were those, when men lived their lives quickly, and then disappeared or were ruined, or committed suicide, and were soon forgotten.

Brabant had gone ashore, and Lester and the second mate—a thin, sallow-faced Chileno named Diaz—were seated under the awning, smoking, and occasionally watching the progress of a small cutter which was about a mile distant, and under the influence of a light air which had sprung up, was heading towards the *Maritana*. She was owned by Dr. Bruce, a planter friend of Lester. His estate was some miles down the coast, and he had been an old shipmate of Lester's ten years before, when Brabant was living in Samoa as manager of the American Plantation Company, and Lester had first made his acquaintance—an acquaintance which had resulted in a firm and lasting friendship. Brabant wanted an overseer—a man who understood the native language—and Lester, then a youth of twenty, and idling about Samoa, waiting a berth as second mate, had been sent to him by an old seafaring friend. For three years they had worked together, and then Brabant, having saved enough money, threw up his shore berth and bought the *Maritana* to resume his former vocation of trader, and took Lester with him as mate, and Diaz, who had also been employed on the plantation, as second mate. That was seven years ago, and the schooner, during that time, had traversed the Pacific from one end to the other over and over again. Sometimes Brabant would take his cargo to San Francisco, sometimes to Singapore, and at rare intervals to Auckland. During one of his ship's visits to Fiji his chief mate found his old friend Bruce settled there as a planter, and Bruce had induced Brabant to make Fiji his head-quarters. So he bought land and built a house, and then, a year before the opening of this story, brought a wife to rule over it, much to the surprise and delight of the white residents of Levuka and the group generally, for John Brabant had always been looked upon as a man whose soul was wrapped up in his extensive business, and as a woman hater. This latter conclusion was arrived at from purely deductive reasoning—he despised and loathed the current idea that living in the South Seas palliated the most glaring licentiousness, and permitted a man to "do as he liked." Therefore he had been set down as a non-marrying man—"an awfully good fellow, but with queer ideas, you know," his many friends would say, and "Bully" Hayes, who knew him well, said that John Brabant was the only clean-living, single man in Fiji, and that if he ever did marry his wife would be "some bony Scotch person of about forty, with her hair screwed up into a Turk's knot at the back of her long head, and with a cold, steely eye like a gimlet. Nine out of ten of good fellows like Jack Brabant do get mated with ghastly wives."

So when the *Maritana* one day sailed into Levuka harbour, and Brabant brought his young wife ashore, the community simply

4

gasped in pleased astonishment, and even the exclusive wives of the leading merchants and planters made haste to call on Mrs. Brabant when they saw in the marriage announcement, published in the Auckland *Herald*, that she was "a daughter of the late General Deighton Ransome, Commander-in-Chief of the Straits Settlements," etc.

In a few months Mrs. Brabant was equally the best-liked and best-hated woman in Fiji—the men paying her the most undivided attention, because she liked it and was Brabant's wife, and the women hating her because she would be, at times, languidly insolent to them, and practically monopolised even the attentions of the naval officers when a dance was given. That nine out of ten of her lady friends detested her merely afforded her secret pleasure— secret, that is, so far as her husband went, for she feared but one thing in the world, and that was that John Brabant would discover her true and worthless nature.

For some minutes the two mates smoked on in silence, then Diaz made a backward gesture towards the bungalow on the hills: "Are you going there to-night?"

Lester nodded. "I think so. He asked me, you see."

The Chileno remained silent for a minute or so, then said, "She is the most beautiful fair woman I have ever seen."

Again Lester nodded, but made no remark. He was well aware that Pedro Diaz shared his dislike for the captain's wife, though he had never openly said so. The Chileno, morose and grim as he was, was intensely devoted to Brabant, who had twice saved his life—once under a heavy rifle fire in the Solomon Islands, when Diaz and his boat's crew were all but cut off and massacred by the natives, and Brabant came out of the fray with a broken arm and a bullet through his shoulder; and once at sea, when he was knocked overboard by the parting of a boom guy, and his captain sprang overboard after him, though the night was as dark as pitch, and the *Maritana* was like to have been smothered by the heavy, lumping seas which fell upon her decks when she was brought to.

"He is a doomed man," resumed the second mate presently, with a sullen yet emphatic tone; "that woman will be his doom. She is beautiful, and as false as she is beautiful. I can see it in her eyes; *he* cannot see. But were I in his place I should not leave her alone. She is not to be trusted."

Lester thought the same, but said nothing, and he and Diaz rose and went on the main deck to welcome Bruce, whose cutter was now coming alongside.

"How are you, Jim? How are you, Mr. Diaz?" said the doctor, a big, bronzed-faced Scotsman with kindly blue eyes, as he sprang over the side and shook hands with them. "I saw the *Maritana* early this morning in tow of the boats, so I started off in the cutter at once. Brabant gone ashore?"

"Yes, about an hour ago," replied the chief mate. "Almost a newly-married man, you see," he added, with a laugh.

Dr. Bruce gave his friend a quick, penetrating glance, but there was no answering smile on his lips. He knew Brabant well, and knew *of* Mrs. Brabant more than did her husband.

The three men sat down under the awning for nearly an hour, smoking and drinking their whiskey-and-soda, and talking freely together. Bruce—much the oldest man of the three—was aware that both his companions were devoted to Brabant, and knew him far better than himself, and so, being a straightforward, purposeful man, he said what he had to say about Mrs. Brabant in very plain language.

"You, Jim, *can* and ought to give him a hint. I can't. If I did he would most likely haul off and knock me down. But he ought to stay ashore this time. She may be only a brainless little fool of a flirt, but there's a lot' of talk about her, especially since that young sweep of a Danvers came here."

"Who is he?" asked Lester.

Dr. Bruce leant back in his seat, and flicked the ash off his cigar. "He's the manager of the new Land and Trading Company here—a little, pretty-faced fellow, with a yellow moustache, curly hair, and as much principle in him as a damned rat. He has the command of any amount of money, and the women here think no end of him. Was in the army—Rifles, I think—but believe, though I can't be sure

6

of it, was kicked out. Thorough beast, but just the kind of man to get along too well with women who don't know him. Now I'll take another whiskey-and-soda after thus traducing Mr. Danvers, who I'm perfectly willing to boot along Levuka beach from one end to the other if he gives me a chance to do it on my own account. And, by Jove, I'll give him a chance to-night."

"Where?" asked Pedro Diaz, with a gleam of sombre light in his dark eyes. 189

The Trader's Wife

"At Manton's. He's sure to come in there about eleven to-night. Goodbye for the present. I'll meet you there about eight."

As the doctor went over the side again the Chilian turned to Lester.

"What did I tell you?" he said gloomily.

## CHAPTER II

AT five o'clock in the afternoon, as Dr. Bruce was seated on the wide verandah of Manton's Hotel, smoking his pipe, and wondering in a lazy sort of a way whether Brabant would hear any of the current scandal about his wife and Danvers, the voice of the latter person broke in upon his musings.

"Hallo, Bruce, how are you?" he exclaimed genially as he sprang up the steps, and extended his hand to the doctor; "I see that Brabant is back."

Bruce answered him curtly enough. "Yes; but you don't know him, do you?"

Danvers clasped his hands over one knee and leant back in his chair. "No; but I see Mrs. Brabant a good deal, and naturally should like to meet her husband. You know him pretty well, don't you?"

"Yes, I do—have known him for nearly ten years." Then he moved his chair slightly so that he might face Danvers. He was not an impulsive man, but as he looked into Danvers's smiling, handsome face the dislike he had always felt towards him, and his keen regard for Brabant, urged him to speak on the subject that was uppermost in his mind, there and then.

"I'm glad I have met you, Captain Danvers," he said quietly, "as I particularly wished to speak to you about a certain matter, and, as you know, I am not often in town."

"Certainly, my dear fellow. What is it?"

"Your question to me just now saves me a lot of explanation. You asked me if I knew Brabant, and I told you that I have known him for ten years. And I must tell you further that he is a man for whom I have the deepest regard and respect. Therefore," and he emphasised the 'therefore,' "you can of course guess the nature of the matter upon which I wish to speak with you."

"'Pon my soul, I can't," and Danvers elevated his eyebrows in pretended astonishment, though his face flushed as he met the doctor's steady, unnerving glance.

Still keeping his eyes on Danvers's face, Bruce went on: "Brabant is a valued friend of mine. He is as unsuspecting and confiding a man as ever lived, but he is a dangerous man to be trifled with. Do you understand me?"

"I'm hanged if I do," replied Danvers, though the angry flash of his clear blue eyes belied his words; "what are you driving at? Just say in plain words what you have to say, and be done with it."

"Right. Plain words. And as few as possible. You have paid Mrs. Brabant such attention that her husband is like to hear of it. Isn't that enough?"

Danvers laughed insolently. "Enough to show me that you are meddling with affairs which do not concern you, Dr. Bruce. I rather imagine that the lady's husband would be the proper person to resent any undue attention being paid by me to his wife—which I deny—than you. Did he commission you to speak to me? I've heard that the Brabant family have always had a strain of insanity running through it."

Bruce started. He knew that what Danvers had said was perfectly true, but had thought that he himself was the one man in Fiji who did know. Brabant had himself told him that several of his family on the father's side had "gone a bit wrong," as he put it.

The contemptuous tone of Danvers stung him to the quick.

"That's a beastly thing to say of a man whose house you visit almost daily—and visit when you have never even met him. You must have been brought up in a blackguardly school."

Danvers sprang to his feet with blazing eyes. "You want to pick a quarrel with me. Very good. I'm your man."

"That's where you are wrong. I don't want to quarrel with you. I wish to warn you. And I tell you again that John Brabant is a dangerous man."

"Are you his deputy? What right have you to interfere in my private affairs?"

"I'm not his deputy; and my interference, if you like to so call it, will certainly save you from a well-deserved kicking. Don't, don't, don't!

No heroics with me, my boy. You haven't a clean record, and *I* know *why* you left the army. Now listen to me. Just put a stop to this business. If you don't, I'll tell both Mrs. Brabant and her husband in your presence that you are not altogether the right sort of man to be accepted as a friend—especially by a young and utterly unsuspicious woman."

Danvers sank back into his seat, white with passion, as Bruce went on relentlessly.

"And I'll tell what I do know of you to every planter and decent white man in the group. I'll make Fiji too hot for you, and your business will go to the deuce. Now, let us have an understanding. Will you put an end to this dallying about after another man's wife? You can do the thing properly, pay a call or two at the house whilst Brabant is at home, and accept general invitations if you like; but——"

"But what?" Danvers's voice was hoarse with suppressed fury.

"Stop visiting Mrs. Brabant whilst her husband is away. No gentleman would act as you have acted. You know what a place this is for scandal. And I believe you have as much of the fool as the *roué* in your mental composition."

"And if I decline to entertain your infernal——"

"Steady. No language, please. If you decline to make me that promise here on the spot, I shall do what I have said—tell husband and wife that you're not the kind of man to receive as a friend."

"And by Heavens, I'll shoot you like a rat."

The doctor rose to his feet, and the two men faced each other—the one outwardly calm and collected, the other shaking with passion.

"What is it to be, Captain Danvers?"

"This, you sneaking Scotch sawbones!" and raising his cane Danvers struck the elder man a savage blow across the face.

In another moment Bruce had closed with him, wrenched the cane from his hand, and drawing back struck him between the eyes with such force that he was sent flying backwards off the verandah, to fall heavily upon the shrubs of the garden beneath, where he lay huddled up in a heap.

A score of people—white and coloured—rushed to the spot. Bruce, carefully standing the cane against the side of the lounge on which he had been reclining, walked down the steps and pushed his way into the little crowd surrounding the fallen man.

"Let me look at him," he said, with grim humour, "as a medical man. I'm afraid I've hurt him more than I intended."

The landlord joined them. "What is the matter, Doctor?"

"Nothing serious, Manton. Ye see, Captain Danvers rang that old gag on me about a surgical operation being necessary for a Scotsman to understand a joke; then I lost my temper and called him a fool, and he tickled me with his cane across my face, and I hit him harder than I intended. But he'll be all right soon. He's only stunned. Carry him into his room."

Manton knew his business. "Just so, Doctor. I'll see to him. But he's given you a fearful bruise on your cheek."

"A mere trifle, Manton," and then without another word he returned to his seat on the lounge, not altogether satisfied with what had happened, and hoping that Danvers would at least have sense enough to corroborate the story he had told Manton as to the cause of the quarrel.

Between seven and eight o'clock Lester and Pedro Diaz came ashore, the *Maritana* being left in charge of the boatswain. By the judicious application of a strip of fresh goat's meat the long bruise on the doctor's cheek had almost disappeared, and he was in his usual placid mood.

"We're a bit too late," remarked Lester, with a laugh, as he and Diaz shook hands; "why couldn't you wait? We heard that you had thrown the new chum Danvers over the verandah an hour or two ago."

Bruce told them the story. "Just as well, Jim. I think he'll take a plain hint that he's sailing on the wrong tack. He went away from here as soon as he came to, and I think will have sense enough to keep away.

Of course there'll be a lot of talk about the row, and Brabant is sure to have already heard of it, but we must stick to the surgical operation yarn. Now settle yourselves for a chat. Touch that bell there."

As the three smoked and talked a pretty Samoan girl appeared on the verandah, holding a note in her hand. She was Mrs. Brabant's maid, and the note was directed to Lester, bidding him, the doctor, and Pedro come up. It was written by Mrs. Brabant herself.

"We must go, Bruce. Your face doesn't look much the worse. Come on."

The walk to Brabant's bungalow took but a few minutes, and both the captain of the *Maritana* and his wife met them at the gate; Brabant looking supremely happy in his quiet way. His wife, however, Bruce at once saw, seemed pale, and spoke her greetings in a hurried, nervous manner, very unlike her usual self.

"What's all the row been about, Bruce?" said Brabant, as they seated themselves on the wide, airy sitting-room. "We heard of it quick enough, I can tell you. My wife seems rather distressed about it, as she quite expected Captain Danvers to call this evening, and I'd like to make his acquaintance."

Bruce gave Mrs. Brabant one swift, sweeping glance which filled her with an undefined terror. Then he laughed.

"Just nothing at all. We quarrelled over what was simply a trifling matter to him, but a good deal to older men like you and I, and that's the whole thing. Now tell me all about the voyage of the *Maritana*."

Brabant saw that there was something beneath the surface, so at once did begin to talk about his voyage; and presently some other people—men and women—dropped in, and the conversation became general, and about ten o'clock Mrs. Brabant, under the plea of a bad headache, bade her guests good-night. She shook hands with some gracious words with Lester and the second mate, but, much to her husband's distress, simply bowed coldly to his friend Bruce, and ignored his proffered hand. The honest, loyal-hearted Scotsman flushed to the roots of his hair, but pretended not to notice the slight.

Long after midnight, when all his guests except Bruce and Lester and his fellow-officer had gone home, Brabant and they walked to and fro under the coco-palms which surrounded the bungalow. Brabant talked most. He was full of future trading schemes, and outlined his plans to his two officers freely.

"It's a bit awkward this affair happening between you and Danvers," he said to Bruce, "for I've had letters from his principals in Sydney which possibly points to a combination of their business and mine as one company, with myself at the head of affairs."

"My row with Danvers won't affect that, Brabant. I know that he represents people in Australia with any amount of money at their backs, and you are the one man in the Pacific to make a 'combine,' as the Yankees say, and found a trading company that will wipe the Germans out of the Pacific. But, apart from business, don't have anything to do with Danvers. He's no good."

"No good?"

"Not a straight man outside of business—not to be trusted. You can tell him I said this of him if you care to do so."

Brabant stopped in his walk, and Lester and Pedro Diaz drew aside a little.

"There must be something wrong about him, Bruce, else I am sure you would not speak as you do. We four are all old friends. Speak freely."

"That's just the thing I cannot do, Brabant. I don't like him, and can only repeat what I have said just now—he's not a straight man—not a man I would bring into my house as a *friend!* Now I must be going. Good-night, old fellow. I'm off again to my place in the morning."

Brabant took his outstretched hand. "Goodnight, Bruce. I wish there were more outspoken men like you in the world. *I under stand.*"

He spoke the last two words with such a look in his deep-set eyes, that Bruce felt that he did at least understand that Captain Danvers was not a man to be trusted—outside of business matters.

## CHAPTER III

About a week after Dr. Bruce had returned to his plantation Brabant and his wife were talking in their dining-room, from the wide-open windows of which the little harbour of Levuka lay basking in the fervid glow of the westering sun.

Pipe in mouth, and with a smile on his bronzed, rugged face, Brabant was scanning a heap of accounts which were lying on the table. His wife, seated in an easy-chair near the window, fanned herself languidly.

"You've spent a lot of money, Nell, in five months—nearly a thousand pounds. Two hundred a month is a big item to a man in my position."

"But you are very well off, Jack. You told me yesterday that you will clear three thousand pounds from this last voyage."

She spoke in a petulant, irritated manner, and her brows drew together as she looked out over the sea.

"Just so, my dear girl; but we cannot afford to live at such a rate as two hundred pounds a month."

"I have entertained a great many people." This was said with a sullen inflexion in her voice.

"So I see, Nell. But you need not have done so. We don't want such a lot of visitors."

"It is all very well for you to talk like that, Jack, but you must remember that I have to keep myself alive in this wretched place whilst you are away."

Brabant turned his deep-set eyes upon her. "Did you find it so very dull then, Nell?"

"Yes, I did. I hate the place, and hate the people, and so I suppose I spent more of your money than I should have done had I been living anywhere else."

"Don't say 'your money,' Nell. I am only too happy to know that I am able to meet all these bills, heavy as they are; and I want you to enjoy

14

yourself as much as possible. But we cannot spend money at this rate, my girl."

He spoke with a certain grave tenderness that only served to irritate her.

"Am I to live here like the wife of one of the common shopkeepers on the beach—see no one, go out nowhere?"

"As my wife, Nell, I expect you to go out a good deal, and see a lot of people. It gives me pleasure to know that the people here like you, and that you have given all these dances and things. But, Nell, my dear, don't be so lavish. After all, I am only a trader, and it seems rather absurd for us to spend more money than any one else does in the matter of entertaining people who, after all, are merely acquaintances. You see, Nell, I want to make money, make it as quickly as I can, so that we can go home to the old country and settle down. But we can't do it if we live at the rate of two hundred pounds a month."

"But if you amalgamate your business with that of Captain Danvers's company, you will make £25,000."

"But I may not amalgamate with Captain Danvers's company, Nell. I am quite satisfied that they can pay me the £25,000, but I am not satisfied as to the *bond-fides* of the company. Danvers himself admitted to me that it is proposed to float the new company in London at a figure which represents four times the value of my own and his own company's properties. I don't like it, Nell. My business as it stands I could sell to the Germans for £20,000, cash down. But I won't associate myself with an enterprise that is not absolutely fair and square, for the sake of an extra £5,000."

"I suppose Dr. Bruce has prejudiced you against Captain Danvers."

"Bruce! No, certainly not, Nell. Why should he? Bruce has nothing to do with the thing. He quarrelled with Danvers over some matter that has nothing to do with me, and Danvers got the worst of it. Certainly, however, before I decide to sell my business to Danvers's company I shall consult Bruce."

"Why consult him?"

"Because he is a man in whose business judgment I have great faith. And he's an honest man."

"And you think Captain Danvers is not?"

"Not at all. But I do think that Captain Danvers attaches an exaggerated value to the prospects of the new trading company. He's very young, you see, Nell, and takes too rosy a view of everything. And I'd rather die in poverty than be the indirect means of making money at the expense of other people. I'm old-fashioned Nell, and when I die, I want to die with the knowledge that I have left a clean sheet behind me."

Nell Brabant rose with an angry light in her eyes. "I hate talking about money and such horrid things. But I do hope you will come to terms with Captain Danvers and his company."

"Wait a moment, Nell. I want to tell you something which I think will please you. Would you like a trip to Sydney?"

"Very much indeed," she answered, with sudden graciousness.

"Well, I'm thinking of sending the *Maritana* there, to be docked and to be overhauled, with Lester in command. Then whilst you are away I shall charter the *Loelia*, cutter, and make a trip through the Line Islands. You will have at least two months in Sydney, and Lester will take good care of you on the voyage."

"It will be a nice change for me, Jack? But why cannot you come?"

"I must make this cruise through the Line Islands before I decide to sell out to Danvers's company."

That evening Brabant announced his plans to his chief officer, and a week later both the *Maritana* and the *Loelia* were ready for sea. During this time Captain Danvers was an occasional visitor to the bungalow on the hill, but he and Brabant met very frequently in the town to discuss business together, and it soon became known that the latter either intended to sell out to, or amalgamate with, the Danvers company.

Ten days before the *Maritana* left Brabant bade his wife goodbye, for the *Loelia* was to sail first. He kissed her but once, and looked so searchingly into her eyes as he held her hand that every vestige of colour left her cheeks.

"You must try and enjoy yourself," he said. "Minea" (her Samoan maid) "and you will be very comfortable on board. You'll have the entire cabin to yourselves, as Lester will take up his quarters in the deck-house."

Half an hour later he was giving Lester his final instructions.

"You will not leave Sydney till either you hear from me or see me. I may follow you in the *Loelia* in a month. But no one else is to know this—not even Mrs. Brabant."

"You may depend on me," replied Lester.

"I know it well. Goodbye, Lester."

---

That evening the *Loelia* sailed from Levuka. Pedro Diaz had been transferred from the *Maritana* and was now mate of the cutter.

As night came on, and the green hills of Ovalau Island changed to purple, Brabant turned suddenly to his officer.

"Come below, Pedro, I want to talk to you."

The Chileno followed him in silence, and the two men remained conversing in almost whispered tones for some time.

"Tell me," asked the Chileno, fixing his dark eyes on the captain's face; "when did you first begin to suspect?"

"From the very first day that I saw her and Danvers together. He betrayed himself—fool that he is—by being too formally polite to her, before me."

"And then you read this letter of his to her. How did you get hold of it?"

"I was coming back from my bathe in Totoga Creek about six in the morning. Went into Manton's for a few minutes' rest and a smoke. Danvers's door was open, and though he was not in the room, I could hear his voice talking to Manton. I stepped inside to sit down and wait for him. He had been writing a letter, which was but half finished. It was to my wife, and began, 'My darling Helen.'"

"Ah-h-h!" said Diaz, in a savage, hissing whisper.

"I left it there, strolled out into the dining-room where Manton and Danvers were having their morning coffee. I joined them, and chatted with them for half an hour. Then I went home, and told Minea what to do when the letter came. It was delivered by Danvers's native servant. Minea met him at the garden gate. He asked if I was in. She said I was out; he gave her the letter, and told her to give it to her mistress, who was still in bed. The girl brought it to me to where I was waiting. I opened it, took a copy of it, and gave it back to her to give to her mistress."

He paused, and then smiled grimly at the Chileno. Then he smoked on in silence.

"You will kill them both?" asked Diaz.

"I don't think so, Pedro. I must wait. And you will stand to me?"

The officer's hand met his in a steady grip.

"That is all for the present, Pedro. She—and he, too—thinks that the Loelia will not be back in Levuka for three months. But we shall be here in less than a month. And if I find that Danvers has gone to Sydney in the monthly steamer, then I shall know how to act," and he tapped the copy of the letter that was in his breast pocket.

Then Pedro told him the real cause of the quarrel between Dr. Bruce and Danvers. Brabant heard him with an unmoved face. "I thought as much," he said briefly.

A few days later, the Loelia, instead of laying northwards for the Line Islands, was at anchor in Apia Harbour in Samoa, and Brabant, leaving the vessel in charge of his mate, paid a round of visits to several of his old friends in various parts of the island. At the end of three weeks he returned on board as calm as usual, and told Diaz to heave up anchor. By sunset that evening the Loelia was sailing between the islands of Savaii and Manono, and heading due west for Fiji before the strong south-east trade wind. Just four weeks from the date of her departure she re-entered Levuka harbour, and the first news that Brabant heard was that the *Eagle*, the monthly steamer to Sydney, had sailed a few days previously, and that among her passengers was Captain Danvers, who had "been called to Melbourne on matters connected with his business," but would be returning in a couple of months. He had left a letter for Brabant, in which, after speaking of company matters, he said: "I do hope I shall have the pleasure of seeing Mrs. Brabant in Sydney before she leaves. I daresay I can get her address from your agents there." As he was reading his letters Bruce came on board.

"You are back sooner than you thought, Brabant."

"Yes. When I got to Samoa I met a German brig bound to the line Islands, and arranged with her captain to see all my traders for me, as the *Loelia* is as leaky as a basket. I'm going to give her a good overhaul here."

There were of course the usual sneering comments made by the local female gossips on Captain Danvers's sudden departure for Sydney, so soon after Mrs. Brabant had left in the *Maritana*. If Brabant knew of them he took no heed. He went about his work as usual, met his friends, and attended to the *Loelia's* repairs in his methodical manner.

Eight weeks passed by, and then the *Eagle*, a slow-crawling old ex-collier, which did duty as a mail and passenger steamer, entered the port, and Danvers, jauntier and handsomer than ever, stepped ashore and took up his old quarters at Manton's Hotel. Here he soon learnt the reason of Brabant's early return, and in less than an hour he was up at the bungalow, and seated opposite Nell Brabant's husband, whom he had found reading his letters.

"I met Mrs. Brabant quite a number of times," he said effusively; "she was looking very well, but I think was getting tired of Sydney when I last saw her. Said that she thought that Fiji after all was the best place, you know."

Brabant nodded. "Just so. Well, we'll see her before another couple of months, I hope."

"I hope so," said Danvers genially, as he raised his glass of brandy-and-soda and nodded "good luck" to his host.

"I was thinking, Danvers," said Brabant, as he laid down unopened the rest of his letters, "that it would be just as well if you came round with me in the *Loelia* and saw my stations in the New Hebrides. It would facilitate matters a good deal, and the cutter is all ready for sea. In anticipation of your coming I have fitted up your quarters on board."

"Delighted, my dear fellow. When do you propose sailing?"

"As soon as ever you like."

"To-morrow, then. I'm anxious to get this matter pulled through. As you will see by your letters from my people, they are prepared to pay ten thousand down at once, and fifteen thousand in three bills, at one, two, and three years."

"That is all right. Shall you be ready tomorrow, then?"

"Quite."

After Danvers had gone to his hotel Brabant went on board the *Loelia*, and he and Pedro Diaz again talked together.

---

At nine o'clock next morning the cutter Loelia weighed anchor, and made sail for "a cruise among the New Hebrides. With Captain Brabant" (so said the tiny weekly newspaper published in Levuka) "was Captain Harold Danvers, who is making a tour of inspection of the captain's properties before taking possession of them on behalf of the new Trading Company."

---

Forty-eight hours after leaving Levuka the cutter was clear of the land, and leaping and spinning before the trade wind which was blowing lustily. Danvers, as he sat in a deck-chair smoking a cigar, took a lazy interest in the crew, who were all natives of the Line Islands—short, square-built, half-naked savages, with jet-black hair and huge pendulous ear-lobes filled with coiled-up leaves. There were but eight of them—the *Loelia* was a vessel of ninety tons—and Diaz was the only white man on board except Brabant and Danvers.

It was four o'clock in the afternoon. A native seaman struck eight bells and Brabant came on deck. Pedro was standing aft beside the helmsman.

"We're going along at a jolly good pace, are we not — —" began Danvers. Then his voice failed him suddenly, and his face turned white as he saw that Brabant was looking at him with the deadliest hatred in his eyes.

"What is the matter with you, Brabant? Why do you — —"

Brabant raised his hand, and Pedro came and stood beside him, and then two of the wild-looking crew suddenly sprang upon Danvers, seized him by the arms, and handcuffed him.

"Away with him below," said Brabant, turning on his heel and walking aft.

Too utterly astounded to offer any resistance, Danvers was hurried along the deck to the main hatch and made to descend. The hold was empty, but an armed native was there awaiting the prisoner.

Diaz followed him below.

"You are to make no noise, nor speak to the sentry," he said, with a sullen savageness; "if you do I shall put on the hatches."

Danvers was no coward, but his heart sank within him. "Is this a joke, or has Captain Brabant gone mad?"

The Chileno looked at him with blazing eyes, and half raised his hand as if to strike. Then, without a word, he turned away and went on deck.

Brabant was seated on the skylight with an outspread chart before him.

"Keep her S.S.W., Pedro. We are steering for Hunter's Island. Set the squaresail."

---

For five days the *Loelia* steered steadily before the trade wind, till one morning there lay before her a huge, treeless cone, whose barren, rugged sides rose blackly from the sea.

Not a vestige of vegetation was visible anywhere from the cutter, and from the summit of the cone, and from long, gaping fissures in the sides, ascended thin, wavering clouds of dull, sulphurous smoke. Here and there were small bays, whose shores showed narrow beaches of black sand, upon which the surf thundered and clamoured unceasingly. Not even a wandering sea-bird was to be seen, and the only sound that disturbed the dread silence of the place was the roar of the breakers mingling with the muffled groanings and heavings of the still struggling and mighty forces of Nature in the heart of the island—forces which, ninety-five years before, had found a vent and destroyed every living thing, man and beast, in one dreadful outburst of flame, whose awful reflection was seen a hundred leagues away.

It was a place of horror and desolation, set in a lonely sea, appalling in appearance to the human eye.

But at one point on the western side, as the *Loelia* crept in under the lee, there opened out a small bay less than fifty fathoms in width from head to head, where, instead of the roaring surf which beat so fiercely against the rest of the island, as if it sought to burst in its rocky walls and extinguish for ever the raging fires hidden deep down in its heart, there was but a gentle swell which broke softly upon a beach less dismal to the eye than the others. For instead of the black volcanic sand the shore was strewn with rough boulders of rock, whose sides were covered in places with a thick, green creeper. Above, the sides of the mountain showed here and there a scanty foliage, low, stunted, and dull tinted; and in the centre of the beach a tiny stream of fresh water trickled through sand and rock and mingled itself with the sea.

Abreast of this spot the cutter's jib-sheet was hauled to windward. Then the boat was lowered and filled with provisions in cases and casks, and Diaz, with four hands, went ashore and carried everything up beyond high water-mark. Brabant watched them unconcernedly from the ship.

The boat returned and Diaz came on deck, and looked at the captain expectantly. Brabant made a gesture towards the main hatch, then stepped forward. Diaz, with two seamen, descended the hold. In two minutes they reappeared with Danvers, who, the moment he came on deck, looked wildly about him.

"For God's sake, listen to me!" he said hoarsely to the Chileno. "Are you, too, and these men, as mad as your captain, or am I mad myself? Where is he? Let me see him. What are you doing with me?"

No answer was made. The native sailors seized him by the arms and dragged him to the side. Then he was lowered into the boat, which at once pushed off and was headed towards the land. He looked, with horror in his eyes, at the dreadful aspect before him, then turned his face towards the cutter. Brabant was leaning on the rail watching him.

The five grim, silent men landed him on the beach, and Diaz pointed without a word to the pile of stores, and then, grasping his steer-oar, motioned to his crew to push off.

"You devils! You fiends incarnate! Are you going to leave me here to die alone in this awful place?" cried Danvers, as with clenched and uplifted hands he saw Diaz swing the boat's head seaward.

The Chileno turned his face slowly towards him.

"You shall not die alone, Señor Danvers. You shall have company — good company."

## CHAPTER IV

One evening Captain Lester of the *Maritana,* then lying in Sydney harbour "awaiting orders," called on Mrs. Brabant at the Royal Hotel.

"I have just received this from Captain Brabant, madam," he said with studied, but cold politeness, as he handed her a letter.

She took it with an impatient gesture. "A letter to you and none to me! Surely he must have written, and the letter has miscarried."

"No doubt, madam," replied the captain of the *Maritana* in the same stiff tones.

Mrs. Brabant motioned him to a seat as she read the letter, first telling Minea, the Samoan maid, who was present, to leave the room. The girl obeyed, and as she passed Lester she gave him such a curious but friendly glance, that now for the first time he began to have a suspicion that she was not false to her master. Then, too, it suddenly flashed across his mind that according to Samoan custom, unknown to her mistress, Minea was a "sister" to Brabant, who had exchanged names with her father, a minor chief of a good family, on whose land Brabant had settled when he first came to Samoa. That alone, he knew, would ensure the girl's unswerving loyalty and devotion to her "brother" — she could not conceal from him anything that affected his honour or reputation.

"She'll tell him," he thought, as he watched Mrs. Brabant read the letter; "thank God I shall be spared the task."

Brabant's letter to Lester was very short. It was dated from Vavau, Friendly Islands, and was as follows: —

*"Dear Lester, — I send you this hurried note by the Tongan Government schooner Taufaahau. I am here in the Loelia, inspecting my stations in connection with their transference to Captain Danvers's company. He is very anxious to realise his ideal, and I do not wish to keep him waiting. If Mrs. Brabant is not in Sydney when this reaches you, please communicate with her as quickly as possible. No doubt she will be quite anxious to return to Fiji now, and I shall be here awaiting*

24

*the Maritana. I hope to see you within three weeks after you receive this. Make the Maritana sail for all she is worth.*

*"Yours sincerely,*

*"John Brabant."*

She handed him the letter. "Thank you, Captain Lester. When do you propose sailing?"

"I am ready for sea now, madam. I only await your pleasure."

He did not look at her as he spoke, for he feared that the hatred and contempt with which he regarded her would show itself in his face.

"I can come on board to-morrow. Will that do?" she asked.

"Certainly, madam, if it will not hurry you too much."

"Not at all, Captain; I am sick of Sydney, and am only too glad to come on board the *Maritana* again." She spoke with a friendly warmth, but Lester's distantly polite manner gave her no encouragement.

"Will you not stay and dine with me?" she asked, with a smile; "do say yes. I feel quite angry that my husband has not written to me. I am really a deserted wife. Don't you think so, Captain Lester?"

Her forced pleasantry was thrown away.

"I am very sorry, Mrs. Brabant, but as we are to sail to-morrow, I must hasten on board at once. There are many matters to which I must attend."

He rose and bowed stiffly, and Nell Brabant extended her hand. He touched it, and in another moment was gone. She sank back in her chair with a white face and terror in her eyes. What did he mean by his cold and distant manner? Did he suspect anything? Did he know anything? How could he? Minea alone knew that she had left Sydney for a month with Danvers, and Minea would not betray her! What need to fear anything?

Then, satisfied with her own powers of intrigue, she smiled to herself, and dismissed Lester's cold face and unresponsive manner from her mind.

When Lester went on board again he took from his pocket a second letter from Brabant, which was marked "Private and Confidential," and with a puzzled brow read it over again. "I want you, Lester, to attend carefully to my instructions. *You are to consider my other letter as cancelled.* I wish you, instead of coming to Tonga, to make all possible haste to 22 10' S. and 170 25' E. I shall meet you there or thereabouts in the *Loelia.* — Yours sincerely. J. B."

"What does all this mystery mean, I wonder?" he muttered, as he looked at an outspread chart on the table; "why should he pick upon the vicinity of such a God-forsaken spot as Hunter's Island for a rendezvous? But it's none of my business." Then he turned in and slept.

---

Sunset in the South Seas.

The *Loelia* was lazily head-reaching towards Hunter's Island, about six miles distant, its grim and rugged outlines showing out clearly under the yellow streaks of the sinking sun, Pedro Diaz was on deck, drinking his coffee, when the native seaman who was on the lookout cried—

"Sail ho, sir! Away there on the weather beam."

Diaz stepped below to Brabant, who was lying in his bunk reading a book.

"Here she is, sir."

"Ah! three days sooner than I expected her, Pedro. You know what to do, don't you? Here is the letter for Lester. Get away as quickly as you can. The night will be fine and clear, and there will be no need to hoist a light for you."

He handed the officer a letter addressed to "Captain James Lester, schooner *Maritana,*" and then rose and began to dress himself.

In a few minutes the cutter's boat, with Pedro Diaz and four hands, was pulling towards the *Maritana* which was coming along under a six-knot breeze. The moment the boat left the side Brabant set the gaff topsail and square-sail, and headed the Loelia towards the north end of the island. Just as she disappeared from the view of those on board the approaching vessel, Pedro Diaz came within hailing distance. He stood up.

"*Maritana* ahoy!"

Lester's voice replied to his hail, the schooner was brought to the wind, the boat ranged alongside, and Diaz ascended.

"How are you, Lester?" he said, shaking hands with his friend. "I have no time to talk. Read this letter at once, and let me get away with all speed."

Lester was impressed with the emphatic manner in which he spoke, and without a single question opened Brabant's letter. Then an exclamation of astonishment burst from him.

"What does it all mean, Pedro? I——"

The Chileno waved his hand impatiently, and shrugged his shoulders. "We must obey orders, Lester."

"Of course. I shall let Mrs. Brabant know at once." Then he read the letter a second time.

"*Dear Lester,—Please ask Mrs. Brabant to get together some of her luggage as quickly as possible, and come on board the Loelia, which is the better vessel of the two as far as comfort goes. Minea can remain on board the Maritana. You will find further orders awaiting you at Levuka.*"

That was all. Lester stepped below, and found his passenger seated at the cabin table.

"That vessel is the *Loelia* madam, and Diaz has just come aboard with this letter;" and he handed it to her.

"What an extraordinary thing! Why did not my husband come for me himself if he is so anxious for me to join him on the *Loelia*. Is she close-to?"

"Yes, but not in sight. I think Captain Brabant was afraid of the wind failing, and the cutter drifting in on the weather side of the island, for he has gone round to the lee side."

Calling Minea, Mrs. Brabant hurriedly packed some necessary clothing, telling the girl the reason for such haste, and in a few minutes she sent word on deck that she was ready. Diaz was already in the boat, steer-oar in hand, and talking to Lester, who was leaning over the rail, wondering why his former comrade seemed so embarrassed, and impatient to get away.

Mrs. Brabant held out her hand. "Good-bye, Captain Lester. I hope you will have a quick passage to Levuka. Goodbye, Minea."

She descended the ladder into the boat, and took her seat, Diaz lifted his hat, and then gave the word to push off.

"Good-bye, Pedro," said Lester.

The Chileno looked up.

"Good-bye, Jim, old comrade."

The men stretched to their oars, and the whaleboat shot out towards the dark shadow of the island as the crew of the *Maritana* went to the braces, the yards swung round, and she stood away to the eastward, and Lester, with a strange feeling of unrest oppressing him, leant with folded arms upon the rail, and wondered why Pedro Diaz had given such a tone of sadness to his last words.

The night was clear with the light of myriad stars, as the boat swept through the gently heaving sea. Diaz, standing grim and sombre-faced at the steer-oar, had not spoken a word since the boat left the ship. His eyes looked straight ahead.

Mrs. Brabant had never liked the dark, sullen-faced Chilian, but now there came into her heart such a sudden, horrible feeling of loneliness that she felt she would be glad to hear him speak.

"Is my husband quite well, Mr. Diaz?"

"Quite well, madam," he replied, still staring straight before him.

His voice appalled her, and she made no further effort to break the dreadful silence as she looked at the black bulk of the island, along whose fissured sides there every now and then ran ragged sheets of smoky flame. The boat rounded the island, and then when opposite the little bay, Diaz swung her head round, and headed directly for the shore.

"Are we landing here?" asked the woman in a faint, terrified voice.

"Yes."

The boat touched the shore, the crew jumped out, carried Mrs. Brabant's two boxes to the beach, placed a lighted boat-lantern on one, and then Diaz silently held out his hand to assist her on shore.

She stepped out, and then stood facing him for a moment, her cheek showing the pallor of deadly fear. Then the seaman thrust his hand in the breast of his coat, and handed her a letter. In another instant, without a word of farewell, he had leapt into the boat again, which at once pushed off—and she was alone.

---

When daylight broke it revealed two figures on the lonely beach—one a woman, who lay prone upon the ground, and wept in silent anguish, and the other a man, whose frightful aspect made him look scarcely human. He was kneeling beside one of the boxes, glaring with the eyes of one almost mad with horror at a letter he had taken from the woman's hand when he discovered her lying unconscious.

*"I have known everything from the very first. Danvers said in one of his letters to you that life with you would be happiness unutterable, even in a desert place. I have brought you here to meet him. He has waited long.*

*"John Brabant."*

And never again were Danvers and Nell Brabant seen by men, and John Brabant and the *Loelia* and her crew were supposed to have been lost at sea.

Ingram Content Group UK Ltd.
Milton Keynes UK
UKHW010849060623
422954UK00001B/239

9 798211 258372